Lolo

DAVID D. VELAZQUEZ

To order additional copies of this book, contact:
Xlibris
844-714-8691
www.Xlibris.com
Orders@Xlibris.com

ISBN: Softcover   978-1-6641-9117-4
        EBook   978-1-6641-9116-7

Print information available on the last page

Rev. date: 08/23/2021

Lolo is a smart, Brave,
Curious, and Creative little girl,
who had an amazing
Dream: to Play guitar for
the whole wide world!

So she saved the money she had earned from doing many-a-chore

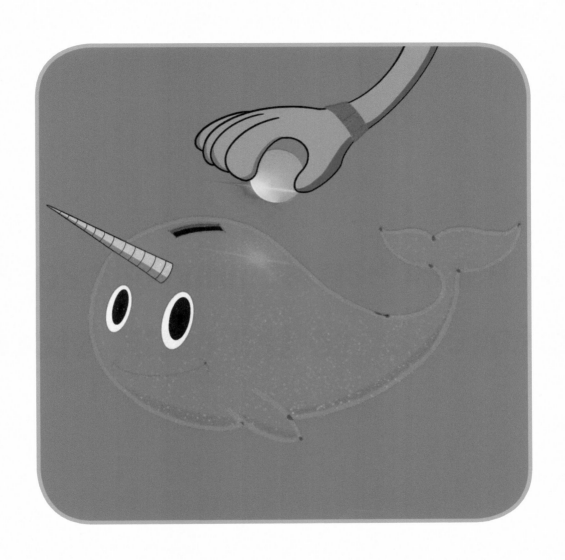

And asked her Mommy and Poppy to take her to the music store!

The music store was full of many wonderful instruments:

ukeleles with tones

happy and sweet

Drums that make you shake your Body and move your feet

Pianos with their full and harmonious sound

As well as Basses that could very well rumble the ground!

So many choices But
so, so little time

But Lolo had already
made up her mind:

She saw an amazing and
sparkly purple guitar

And she knew immediately
it was the one that would
make her a star!

The sound it made, the way
it felt in her hands...

For Lolo it was easy to imagine

she was on stages in
faraway lands!

Playing guitar came straight

from Lolo's heart

And nothing in this Planet

could stop her from

making her art!

CPSIA information can be obtained
at www.ICGtesting.com
Printed in the USA
BVHW020157310821
615682BV00002B/18